TopGear

BEST BITS

The Challenges

BBC Children's Books
Published by the Penguin Group
Penguin Books Ltd, 80 Strand, London WC2R 0RL, England
Penguin Group (Australia) Ltd, 250 Camberwell Road,
Camberwell, Victoria 3124, Australia (a division of Pearson
Australia Group Pty Ltd)
Canada, India, New Zealand, South Africa

Published by BBC Children's Books, 2008
Text and design © Children's Character Books, 2008

10 9 8 7 6 5 4 3 2 1

Written by Jason Loborik
Designed by John Fordham

ISBN: 978-1-40590-458-2

Printed in China

After 47 years,
I've **never** been
speechless!

Contents

This is just the **happiest** car in the world. I shall call it **Oliver**... I wish I hadn't said that!

It's **slow** but certain, and I'm **not** sinking!

Introduction

Welcome to the Top Gear Challenges! Never let it be said that Top Gear isn't about attempting the impossible. Over the next few pages you'll find that no matter how bizarre, weird, or frankly stupid the challenges handed to them, Jeremy, Richard and James will always triumph – even if they get really irritable and call each other names.

We had a look at all the amphibious cars from the past and were baffled why everyone reckons they're so tricky to build. What's so hard? You take your favourite car, stick a whopping outboard motor on it and drive into the water.

NASA may spend billions of dollars on their space shuttles, but we do just as well with an old Robin Reliant, a few boffins in a shed, a budget of about £5.50 and pure grit and determination.

FFOOOM

Even the most boring vehicle known to man gets its comeuppance. We hack off the roof of a people carrier and replace it with our own homemade canvas soft-top that somehow manages to be both stylish, yet practical. Kind of.

And as for the biggest, most epic challenge of all... we prove beyond all doubt you can trek across Africa in the most clapped-out, half-wrecked, rear-wheel drive car possible. We actually laughed at the challenge of racing 1000 miles across muddy bogs, sand banks and fast-flowing river, to be back in time for Sunday's show without so much as a hair out of place. And yes, we're referring to the best and worst hairdo's on television – Richard's and James'.

So, as you'll see, there's simply no challenge we can't handle.

Faster, Higher, Stronger... Power!

Trekking Across Africa

Richard, James and Jeremy get packed off to Africa with just £1,500 each to buy a car. The guys have got to get their cars all the way from east to west across the African country of Botswana. It's a thousand miles of all kinds of rough and dangerous terrain, so they'd each better get something good!

James' Mercedes

James has bought a 1985 Mercedes-Benz 230E. He reckons that Africans love it because it's comfortable, rugged and reliable. Everything in it seems to work, apart from the handbrake!

> You need a car like this that can be mended with a **brick** and a piece of **string!**

Jeremy's Lancia Beta

Jeremy's bagged himself a 1981 Lancia Beta Coupe. He remembers Lancia building some tough rally cars in the past, but reckons they forgot everything the day they made this Beta. Everything's broken, including the steering and gearbox, and it's overheating even before they set off!

> That's normal isn't it, that **fizzing?**

Richard's Opel Kadett

Richard's bought the oldest car of all, and it's the same age as James! It's a 1963 Opel Kadett and cost £1,200 – a proper bargain. The brakes are terrible though and it originally had just 40 horsepower. How much will it have left after all these years?

You've both been **idiots.** Brilliantly interesting, brilliantly stylish, but **stupid!**

This is just the **happiest** car in the world. I shall call it **Oliver**... I wish I hadn't said that!

They're off!

The guys put their car worries to the back of their minds and zoom off. It's pretty good going at first, with a nice, smooth tarmac road. It's early morning and they've not been on the road long, when Jeremy suddenly turns into Bill Oddie and does a spot of bird-watching. Hang on, shouldn't they do a few more miles before they stop for a break?

You tick them off when you've seen them. Hornbill, southern yellow-billed...

Rough going

It's been easy so far, but it's a different story when the tarmac suddenly runs out! The going gets rougher and more dusty. It all gets too much for Oliver and he conks out after just half a mile! Richard fiddles madly with the engine and electrics to try and get it going.

James and Jeremy think it's hilarious, because if anyone's car stops working altogether, they have to complete the challenge in the dreaded Volkswagen Beetle as punishment!

It is collectively our **least** favourite car in the **world!**

It's a close one, but Richard manages to get it going again.

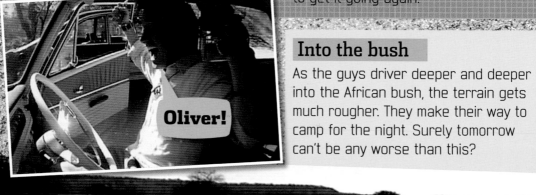

Oliver!

Into the bush

As the guys driver deeper and deeper into the African bush, the terrain gets much rougher. They make their way to camp for the night. Surely tomorrow can't be any worse than this?

Life or death

Next morning, they're told they're going to be the first people to drive cars all the way across the lifeless Makgadikgadi, a vast plane that used to be a lake many thousands of years ago. It might look like good terrain to drive on, but the surface is just a thin, salty crust with oozy mud underneath.

> If you run out of water, you will **die.** If your car breaks down and you can't be rescued, you will **die.** If you run out of food, you will **die...!**

Drastic weight loss

Laughing in the face of death, the guys set about trying to make their cars lighter to prevent them sinking into the ground. Jeremy gets busy with a hammer. But Richard can't bring himself to smash bits off Oliver!

> Thanks awfully!

CRASH!

SMASH! CLUNK!

KSSsH!

Attack from the air

Next morning, they have a friendly visit from the vice-president of Botswana who arrives by air. Smart man. He's shocked when they tell him about their challenge.

> I've just never known **anybody** to go across in a car!

Making tracks

They set off at and it's soon obvious that Jeremy and James might be in trouble. It's not long before James gets completely stuck in the gooey ground. Jeremy tries to help out by giving him a gentle push with the Lancia. No good. So after a fair bit of digging, and the combined strength of the entire Top Gear camera crew, James gets moving again.

Just a **nudge!**

Car bashing (again)

The ground becomes even more boggy, so to avoid being bogged for the 1,000th time, James and Jeremy take a sledge-hammer to their cars once more. The Merc and Lancia are now stripped down to their frameworks, but at least they're not sinking any more! For now, anyway.

KSSSH!

HMV 794 GP

Stick in the mud

They're fooling themselves if they think it's going to be that easy, though. The ground gets sludgier than ever! Only the Opel is trouble-free, which is actually not very good news for Richard because he's the one who has to push the others out of the mud.

URRRRRGHH!

Why don't all cars have no doors? When I come to power I'm going to make it a **rule!**

Desert island

Almost a third of the way across the Makgadikgadi, they stop at Kubu Island. Night's drawing in, and they see the most incredible sunset and are momentarily speechless. Incredible!

Dust storms

Next morning brings a scary warning. Today their problem will be dust, not mud. As James and Jeremy have no windows, they'll have to wear loads of protective gear to make sure they can breathe properly. How bad can a bit of dust be?

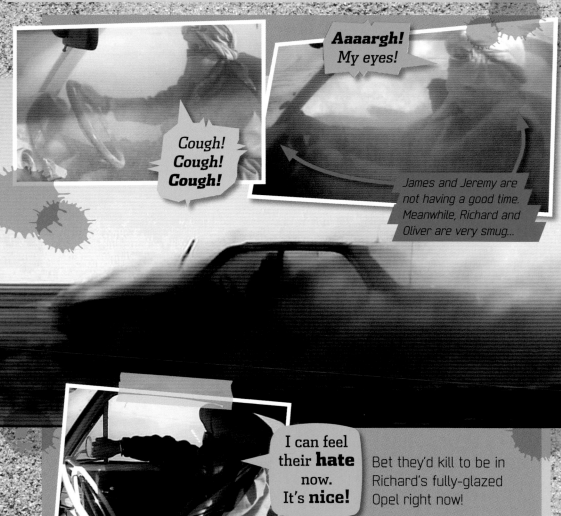

Breakdown

The Lancia's just about had it. It's got no power and no drive, so Jeremy's got a spot of car maintenance to do. And Richard and James leave him to it.

CHUG-CHUG-CHHHHUUUG!

Do you remember what the man said, Jeremy? Break down and you will... what is it? Have a nice time? No. **Die.**

I'm not sure which I favour most here — certain **death** or that **Beetle!**

They've made it!

By some miracle, our brave, battered and somewhat filthy heroes survive the Makgadikgadi. And then they remember that they're not even halfway across Botswana yet.

I think the Makgadikgadi's one of the most **unpleasant** places I've ever been. It's just a big bowl of **dust!**

Will they make it, or will their clapped-out second-hand cars conk out completely? Turn to page 38 to find out!

Building an Amphibious Vehicle

The guys have to each buy a car and have only two days to convert them so they can travel across both land... and water. Will they sink or swim?

Jeremy's Pick-Up

Jeremy's got himself a Toyota Hilux pick-up truck. Why? Well, as previous Top Gear tests have proved, it's completely indestructible. So, getting it across a bit of water should be no problem.

CRASSH

Stick a motor on it!

Jeremy's plan is so simple, it's almost genius. Just grab an outboard motor, stick it on the back of the truck, and off you go.

Cars that swim

Ever seen a car that thinks it's a boat? There have been a few attempts to make amphibious cars in the past. Some worked okay, but of course the Top Gear team plan to build the best amphi-cars ever!

Richard's Camper Van

When it comes to testing the amphi-cars, Richard's got no idea what kind of water they'll have to get across. Hoping it's going to be a river or canal, he plans to make a narrow boat out of a camper van.

> I've bought a camper van which I'm going to turn into a **houseboat.** Of sorts.

James' Triumph Herald

James is determined to triumph in the challenge, but he doesn't plan to use the car's engine to power it. Instead, he's going to use the power of Mother Nature.

> I'm going to fit it with a **mast** and some **sails.** How **brilliant** is that?

Power mad

Jeremy goes to a powerboat expert for advice. His name is Steve. And of course, Jeremy argues with him. Steve thinks a small 2.3 horsepower outboard motor will work nicely, but Jeremy wants two huge 225 horsepower engines, naturally.

Honestly, I want **this!**

You **can't** put two on it! That's half the power of a Formula 1 car!

This is **complicated!**

Bull-bar fight!

Now for the design. Steve insists that the car needs a boat-shaped hull so it can go forward in the water. Eventually, Jeremy sees Steve's point and gives in so it's now time to remove the bull bar. This is a Hilux though and it's not going to give in easily.

FZZZZzHh!!

Ow, I'm on **fire!**

SMASH!

CLUNK! CLUNK!

TOYBOTA

The Damper Van is born

Richard has a vision. He wants his camper van to look as much like a boat as it can. He's going to extend the bow and stern (front and back) and attach a small propeller to the engine. He goes shopping and picks up a chimney, bits of rope, and even a duck.

It doesn't have to be **fast.**

Slice it up!

James is busy, watching as his Triumph is sawn to bits. The hood is hacked off to make way for the mast and sails.

The road test

The guys' first challenge is to drive their amphi-cars to Rudyard Reservoir. Jeremy does fine, but Richard's added a lot of weight to the Damper Van, and it struggles with a lack of power and an overheating engine. James has engine failure too, so he hitches a lift instead.

Making a splash

Will the amphi-cars sink or swim? They've got to race two miles to the other side of the reservoir, and James is the first to take the plunge in his Triumph Herald. All goes well for a few seconds, until he drifts into some weeds on the bank and gets stuck.

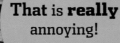

That is **really** annoying!

Toybota floater

Jeremy's next, and the Toybota Hilux manages to stay afloat very nicely. He takes it for a test drive, but goes so fast that water starts sploshing over the Toybota's bow. Will he be able to resist applying the 'power!'?

No, **no, no!** I've got a massive bow-wave at the front!

Damper disaster

Richard's Damper Van is cursed from the start. His propeller breaks on the ramp so he's left drifting with no power. And he might have welded his doors together but hasn't exactly made the van watertight...

Oh no, it's **sinking!** My engine doesn't **work!**

That sinking feeling

In a weak moment, Jeremy offers Richard a spare outboard motor. It keeps failing though, and with gallons of water pouring in, the Damper Van gets damper and damper!

Oh no! It's going, it's **going!**

It's slow but certain, and I'm **not** sinking!

Praying for wind

James is happily waggling the rudder on his Triumph, but try as he might, it's not getting him very far. He really needs a good gust of wind to carry him along, and he just has to sit tight till he gets one!

Rise Toybota! Up, **up!**

A bad move

Jeremy rescues Richard, and even though they're racing James, who's travelling at the slowest speed ever recorded by man, Jeremy still insists on going at top speed. Bad idea.

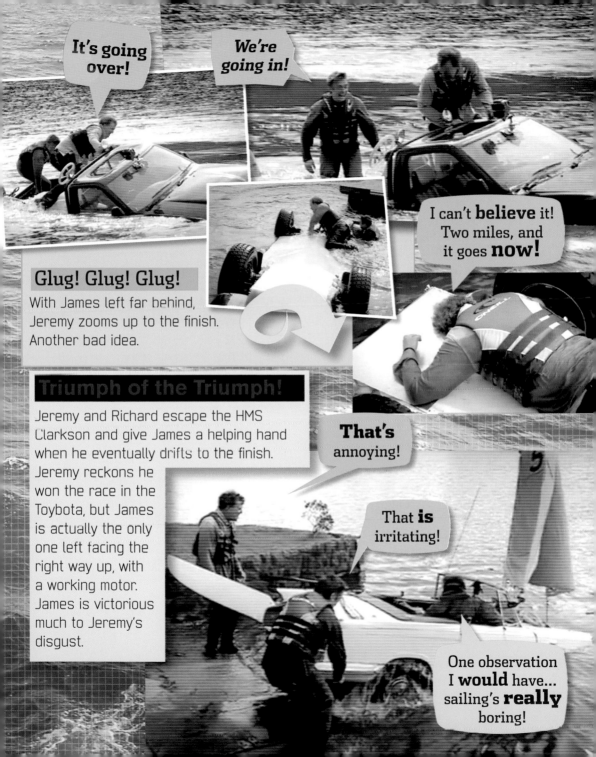

It's going over!

We're going in!

I can't **believe** it! Two miles, and it goes **now**!

Glug! Glug! Glug!

With James left far behind, Jeremy zooms up to the finish. Another bad idea.

Triumph of the Triumph!

Jeremy and Richard escape the HMS Clarkson and give James a helping hand when he eventually drifts to the finish. Jeremy reckons he won the race in the Toybota, but James is actually the only one left facing the right way up, with a working motor. James is victorious much to Jeremy's disgust.

That's annoying!

That **is** irritating!

One observation I **would** have... sailing's **really** boring!

Building a Convertible

Behind the wheel of a car like this, you feel like you're **drowning** in **wallpaper paste!**

How do you make a boring old people carrier into something fun? It's easy. Just hack off its roof, stick on a homemade canvas soft-top, then push it to the limit, with Jeremy, Richard and James in charge.

The people carrier

This is the lucky Renault Espace that's going under the knife. It's not exactly Jeremy's favourite car in the world so he's looking forward to cutting it up.

The big plan

James is in charge and has attempted to draw a detailed plan. He reckons it should be easy to take the roof off without weakening the car at all. The Espace is very long, so he's divided the new fold-down roof into two sections. The back bit is on a frame, with a removable hoop in the middle.

Can this be put up and taken down in under, let's say, a **day?**

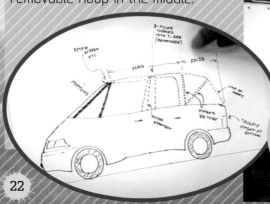

Yeah, a couple of minutes!

Why don't I believe you?

Cutting crew

With safety specs on, they start cutting through the roof's framework. Jeremy's fed up with the electric carving knife James has given him, so he grabs a much meaner-looking tool and gets to work.

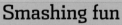

SMASH!

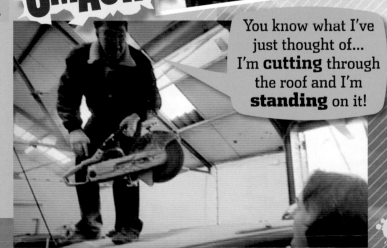

Smashing fun

Richard gets a bit carried away with his sawing and accidentally shatters one of the car windows. Meanwhile, Jeremy seems to have forgotten some basic safety rules.

You know what I've just thought of... I'm **cutting** through the roof and I'm **standing** on it!

Raise the roof

Now for the tricky bit. With all the sawing and window-breaking over, they slowly lift off the roof section and it weighs a tonne!

URRRK!

It's like somebody's Espace has **sunk!**

James, you know you wanted 57 inches wide? The material you bought is **55** inches wide!

I've sewn **myself** to the machine!

Cover up

Now for the new fold-down roof, and time to put James' ingenious plan into action. He's going to make the frame, while Richard's in charge of fastening it to the car. Meanwhile, Jeremy's got the job of sewing the canvas material together.

Tube boob

The disasters don't end there. James has to bend a long tube in two places, as part of the roof framework. It's meant to look a bit like a footy goal when it's finished. Easy, right?

Oh, you **utter** clot!

The speed challenge

With the convertible's roof finally in place, it's time for the first challenge. They've got to drive at a top speed of 100mph with the roof up, without anything breaking or falling off.

ZZOOOOMMM!

VRROOOMM

Breaking up

Richard's drawn the short straw sitting at the back, with the roof collapsing all around him. Jeremy puts his foot down and hits 70mph. The force is so great on the roof that Richard has to hold on to it. If he lets go for just a second the whole lot will blow away. They finally get up to 100mph and that's one challenge finished. Surely the next one can't be worse than this?

Your stitching is **rubbish!**

It's really **not good** back here. It's not good **at all...**

She's breaking up! Come on, you useless piece of junk!

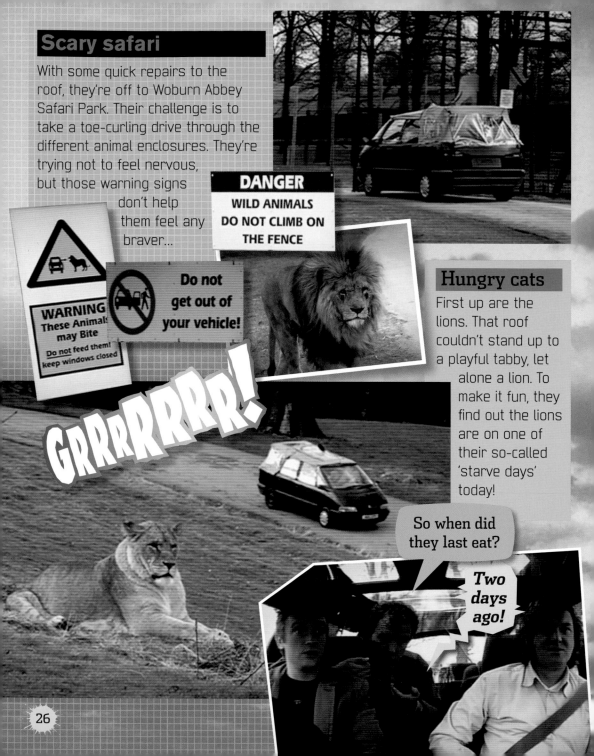

Scary safari

With some quick repairs to the roof, they're off to Woburn Abbey Safari Park. Their challenge is to take a toe-curling drive through the different animal enclosures. They're trying not to feel nervous, but those warning signs don't help them feel any braver...

DANGER
WILD ANIMALS
DO NOT CLIMB ON
THE FENCE

WARNING
These Animals
may Bite
Do not feed them!
keep windows closed

Do not
get out of
your vehicle!

GRRRRRRR!

Hungry cats

First up are the lions. That roof couldn't stand up to a playful tabby, let alone a lion. To make it fun, they find out the lions are on one of their so-called 'starve days' today!

So when did they last eat?

Two days ago!

Monkey magic

Surviving the lions, our brave trio slowly make their way into the monkey enclosure. Suddenly, one of them jumps up at the car and perches on the roof. Time to panic. Jeremy wishes he'd made a better job of that stitching!

Get off!

AAARRRGH!

As part of the challenge, the Top Gear production team has put lots of treats on the Espace's roof. Monkeys suddenly descend, helping themselves to nibbles. Inside the car, the panic level goes up another notch...

Please, can we go?

The final challenge

Relieved that they haven't been ripped to shreds, the guys accept their final challenge. Can they survive a car wash?

Million pound wash

The car wash selected for the challenge cost a million pounds and features the latest technology to deliver the cleaning power of a Category 5 hurricane!

Has anyone else become slightly nervous?

Yes, I'm **terrified!**

Getting wet

The rollers close in and the roof starts to crumple under the pressure. Then, just when they think they might get through this alive, high-pressure water jets blast through the roof and give them a soaking!

PSSSSHHHHH!

URRGH!

I'm wet now!

Abandon ship!

It's no good, the roof's collapsing under the strain and they've got to get out of there! Jeremy's the first to leap out, and the others scramble after him, just as the roof completely folds in on itself!

Get out of the side!

BOOOOM!

Just run!

Fiery finish

You've never seen the guys move so fast without a car! Their worst fears come true when the car wash overloads and catches fire. Oops. Well, winning two challenges out of three isn't all that bad, is it?

Robin Reliant
Space Shuttle

Can James and Richard conquer space using a car your granddad would drive? Why not give it a go?

The challenge

Space rockets cost an absolute fortune – the Americans spend billions of dollars on theirs – but Richard and James reckon you can do it for a lot cheaper if you base your rocket on a car.

The tricky thing is, they want to make a spacecraft that can be used again and again, in other words a space shuttle. So, Richard buys himself the most suitable car he can think of – a Robin Reliant. It's light, it's cheap and it even tapers to a point a bit like a rocket!

Yes, it's been around for **30 years,** and for 29 of those years it's been a complete **joke!**

Meet the boffins

James and Richard get a bunch of rocket experts to help build the shuttle. When they mention they want to get a Robin Reliant into space, the silence is deafening.

Have you got a spare **billion** dollars?!

How will it work?

Deciding it won't actually go as far as outer space after all, they come up with a cunning plan.

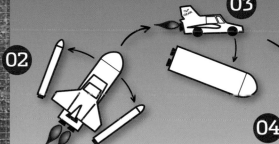

01 The Robin Reliant shuttle is attached to a big rocket that will launch it off the ground.

02 At about 1,000 feet, and travelling at 100mph, the two rocket boosters will empty and fall away.

03 Accelerating to 140mph, the shuttle separates from the main fuel tank.

04 The Reliant comes under the control of the pilot who guides it to the ground.

05 One space shuttle ready for its next voyage.

Doodle time

The big plan's all very well, but Richard's worried. The team reckon they need a huge amount of power just to get the Reliant off the ground so this rocket's going to be massive! They all agree there's no way a person could go up in this. Not even The Stig.

With no one actually on board the shuttle, Richard's next job is to find someone who'll somehow be able to fly it. As he manages to break a window when he flies his model plane, he's obviously not the man for the job. He meets champion model aeroplane pilot Steve Holland, who reckons he can fly it by remote control.

CRASH

AVON Remote Controlled FLYING CLUB

> I was thinking of a **firework** on a stick!

Big boosters!

The shuttle's starting to take shape. Richard's eyes pop out when he sees the rocket booster. There will be two of them as well as an even bigger fuel tank.

> What occurs to me now is the list of things to go wrong...

> ...is **enormous!**

Will it fly?

LAUNCH MINUS 8 DAYS

Richard and James are worried about the shape of their Reliant space shuttle. Even with wings and rocket boosters of its own, will it actually fly? They go and see some aerodynamics experts who test a model of the shuttle in a wind tunnel. The results aren't very encouraging!

More bad news

Steve, the pilot, also builds a model of the shuttle to see how well it will fly. His Reliant detaches itself from the aeroplane and plummets straight down to earth!

LAUNCH MINUS 7 DAYS

It's going to come down like a **lift** with the **cable cut!**

You're **not** filling me with hope, Steve...

Getting it together

Not to be put off, the rocket's finally put together at a military training ground near Newcastle. The main fuel tank is attached to the launch pad together with the rocket boosters. Richard's concerned though that the whole thing might just tip over...

Look it's **fine.** It's held down with some old concrete blocks...

...and some straps that you use to hold furniture down in a removal van!

Bomb disposal

Richard and James have a big job to do. They've got to dig a hole for Steve the pilot to sit in. The thing is, the training ground is littered with unexploded bombs! James arms himself with a cheap metal detector while Richard protects himself with a JCB digger.

LAUNCH MINUS 21 HOURS

I'm not kidding. This bit is **genuinely** very scary!

Risky business

Now for the most dangerous bit so far. The shuttle has to be attached to the rockets and fuel tank. If any of the release mechanisms break, the shuttle won't separate during flight, and the whole lot will drop like a lead balloon.

All set

It's the morning of the launch and the shuttle's finally fitted together. There's a whole load of nervous lip chewing and nail-biting over the next few hours, as the team double-check the intricate on-board electronics and connections. Oh, and they mustn't forget to fill up with fuel either!

LAUNCH MINUS 10 HOURS

3... 2... 1... BLAST OFF!

00:00

Oh, yeah!

Looking good

The shuttle's had a successful lift-off. Richard and James can barely believe their eyes. It's working! In a flash, the rocket boosters break away and fall to earth. Everything's going to plan. What can possibly go wrong now?

Trekking Across Africa

PART 2

They've made it across vast, dusty plains, but our intrepid heroes still have hundreds of miles to go and their cars are in a shocking state. How many more challenges can they take?

Into the desert

The next part of the trek is to cross the Kalahari desert, and the terrain is uncomfortably bumpy.

The rally stage

First, it's time for another challenge. The cars have suffered and now the guys are going to find out how much performance they've lost. Time to meet The Stig's African cousin! First up, it's Oliver, and African Stig puts it through some serious power slides, sending choking clouds of dust everywhere.

Everyone takes away a special memory of the Kalahari... I think, **'bumpiness'**.

Uphill struggle

Next, it's James' car. It doesn't do too badly, but gets stuck going up an incline.

VRRoOoMm

Jeremy's smile disappears when his Lancia starts smoking before it's even set off! He wants to let it cool down, but their rally driver has had enough and walks off. James is declared the winner.

Out of fuel

Once Jeremy's car is fit to drive, the guys discover a new problem. They've hardly got any fuel and it's a 60-mile drive to the town of Maun where they can fill up. Forgetting the long, winding roads, they'll have to drive off-road to save fuel.

James gets stuck, but he has a brainwave. He puts a few stones down for the tyres to grip on to. Amazingly, it works, and he's on his way!

I'm going to make a rudimentary **temporary road** for my back wheel!

Dangerous drive

They make it to Maun, and next morning hear about the most blood-chilling challenge yet. They have to drive through the Okavango Delta, where they will encounter loads of deadly animals including lions, leopards, cheetahs, hyenas, wild dogs, crocodiles... the list is endless. Only one thing to do, James and Jeremy have to protect their half-wrecked cars any way they can.

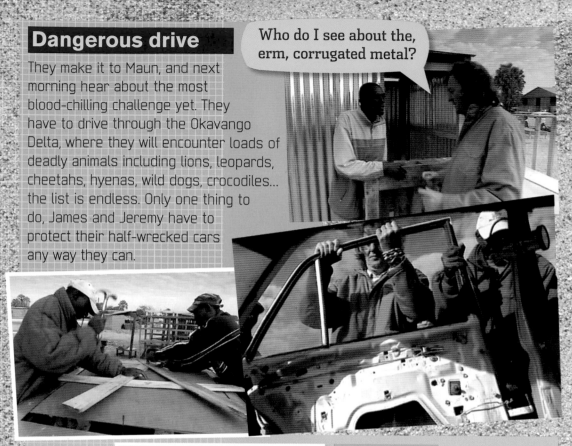

Who do I see about the, erm, corrugated metal?

Odd mods

James does okay. A new wooden roof is fitted and he finds a new boot lid and door that both fit perfectly. While he's not looking, though, Jeremy and Richard chuck in a few mods of their own.

He effectively becomes a **burger van!**

Rickety rides

That afternoon, they set off for the Okavango Delta and the guys are nervous. One of Jeremy's doors is now a gull-wing and the other doorframe is blocked up with tin cans. They'll keep out a ferocious lion, won't they?

> God, this is like being in an allotment **shed** on a very **windy** day!

Driving along, bits of James' Merc start flapping about, and he begins to get a little worried.

Soft sand

On their way to the game reserve the road changes for the worse. The surface is very soft sand, and to stop the cars getting bogged down, they have to drive as quickly as possible.

Bridge bother

Things get even trickier when they come to a rickety wooden bridge. The rally's taken its toll on Jeremy's Lancia – the throttle has become jammed wide open and he can't hold the car back with the brakes.

> **Thanks,** well help yourself to my brakes, **why not?**

> You're gonna have to drive **faster!**

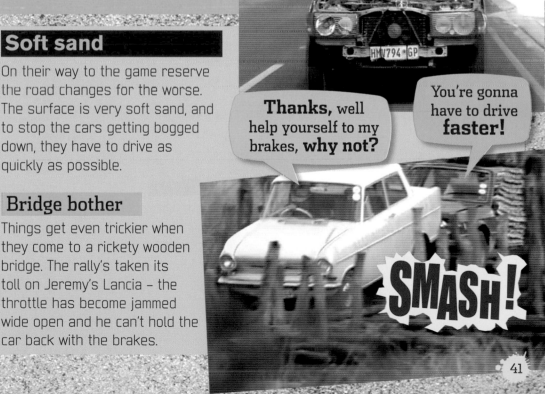

SMASH!

Animal antics

A quick repair job to Jeremy's throttle and they head deeper and deeper into the game reserve, where they see all sorts of amazing wildlife. James even has a go at doing a TV commentary like David Attenborough.

That one's lifting its, sort of, paw up a bit like a **dog!**

The joke's on Richard

That night, they camp by a river and Richard's got another trick to play on James. He's going to grab the rotten, smelly meat from the Merc and put it in James' tent under his bed.

Um, hang on, that's my bag...

...this is **my** tent! Oh man, get it **out!**

Water disaster

Next day, the cars are in a bad way, and they have what seems an impossible task when they find their route blocked by a river. Richard reckons it's too deep, so carries on along the bank, looking for a shallower bit to cross. James and Jeremy take their chances and plunge right in!

It's getting **deeper!**

I've got **water** coming into my car. I've got a **wet bottom!**

A proper crossing?

Meanwhile, Richard's been patient and found himself a proper place to cross. The Opel dives in, but luck isn't on Richard's side today. He soon loses control of the car and water comes gushing in! Amazingly, a local tourist truck passes by and tows the old bathtub out of the river.

Oh, no! **Oh, God!** It's stalled, it's going **down!**

GLUG GLUG

SPLOOSH

43

Can he fix it?

The others manage to make it across the river, but Richard's car has pretty much had it. Richard and a bush mechanic work all night. Oliver's made it this far – and Richard's not going to give up on him without a fight!

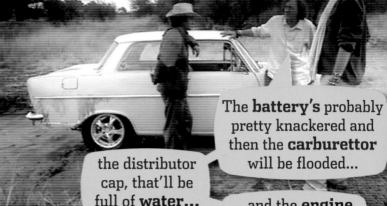

The **battery's** probably pretty knackered and then the **carburettor** will be flooded...

the distributor cap, that'll be full of **water**...

...and the **engine** itself, I mean, if a bit of water went into the **cylinders**...

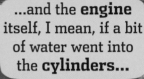

It's a miracle!

The next morning, Jeremy and James' jaws drop when they see the Opel back on the road.

After 47 years, I've **never** been speechless!

44

The final push

With all the cars defying the odds, they push on to the western border. While James' car is going fine, the others are downright dangerous. Richard's got no proper brakes, so has to use his handbrake instead. In the Lancia, every time Jeremy brakes, it veers off to the right and he can't steer left to correct it!

At the end of the Okavango, guess what happens? Yes, the Lancia breaks down. Again. With just 60 kilometres to go, it's Jeremy's turn to feel the threat of the Beetle. But luck is on his side.

It lives!
It lives!

VRROOOMM

REPUBLIC OF NAMIBIA
60

The finish

At last, James and Richard make it to the border. Jeremy's broken down and they've gone on ahead without him. Jezza finally arrives and in true Top Gear spirit, Jeremy, Richard and James argue about whose car is the best.

Realistically, we have to say, the **Lancia's** won it.

Ahhhh. **No.**

By what **possible** measure? It's the **worst!**

Glossary

Aerodynamic – A word often used to describe cars or planes that travel easily through the air, with little resistance. Not really a word that springs to mind when you think of Reliant Robin, but it did with Richard for some reason.

Amphibious – Able to live or operate on land and in the water. The Top Gear cars didn't quite manage this, did they?

Bow – The front end of a boat or ship. Jeremy had a knack for dipping his Toybota's bow into the water all the time, making it sink.

Brake Horsepower (bhp) – The standard measurement of a car's engine power. Obviously, the more horsepower it's got, the quicker it goes! Power, by the way, is a word Jeremy likes shouting more than any other.

Carburettor – A device that mixes together air and fuel in the right amounts, before it goes into the car's engine. Quite useful!

Chassis (say 'shassy') – The car's basic framework which has various different parts fastened to it, such as the engine, the bodywork and the suspension. Not a good idea to go cutting it up, and luckily the guys remembered this golden rule when building their convertible.

Cylinder – Part of a car engine that contains a moving piston. The more cylinders there are in an engine, the more power it's got. (And, of course, the more excited Jeremy gets.)

Distributor cap – A device in the car's ignition system that delivers electricity to the spark plugs.

Makgadikgadi (say 'Ma-caddy-caddy') – Vast, salty planes in Botswana which were once lake beds many thousands of years ago. James hates them because they're dusty and make him cough a lot.

Suspension – The system on a car which uses springs and shock absorbers to give good handling, and also helps prevent the vehicle shaking itself to bits (and your bum scraping along the road).

Stern – The rear part of a boat or ship.

Throttle – A valve which controls the amount of air and fuel going into the engine. The more you press the accelerator, the more the valve opens up, and the faster you go!

Pontoon – A flat-bottomed boat, basically a floating platform. Shame Jeremy never quite reached it in his Toybota!

Rocket booster – A launcher propelled by liquid propellant that powers a spacecraft, aka Robin Reliant, at take-off. The boosters are supposed to fall away after take-off as the spacecraft continues into space. Note how this method spectacularly failed with the Robin Reliant space shuttle challenge.